MW01070580

This book is dedicated to Bart, the love of my life, who brought me the light of Paris that shines forever brightly in my heart.

To Rebecca, who taught me how to feel. I am eternally grateful.

To my children—Sofia, Dean, Ava, and Theodore—who love to get lost in a good book and continuously inspire me to create.

In gratitude,
Maria Castellucci Moore

MASCOT KIDS!
an imprint of Amplify Publishing Group

www.mascotbooks.com

Vivienne in Paris

©2023 Maria Castellucci Moore. All Rights Reserved. No part of this publication may be reproduced, stored in a retrieval system or transmitted in any form by any means electronic, mechanical, or photocopying, recording or otherwise without the permission of the author.

For more information, please contact:
Mascot Kids, an imprint of Amplify Publishing Group
620 Herndon Parkway, Suite 320
Herndon, VA 20170
info@mascotbooks.com

Library of Congress Control Number: 2022905634

CPSIA Code: PREG1122A
ISBN-13: 978-1-63755-143-1

Printed in China

Vivienne in Paris

Maria Castellucci Moore

Illustrated by Emanuela Mannello

*B*onjour! I'm Vivienne. Today was a day unlike any other. I roamed the streets of my city and saw it in a new light. I can't wait to share with you what I discovered . . .

It was a crisp, sun-drenched morning in Paris. The birds were chirping and singing the sweetest melodies. My cue to rise and shine for the day began with church bells ringing throughout the city. Outside my balcony, I could see the bustle of the city streets and the frantic humming of passersby: waves of people, buses, taxis, and bikes, and dogs being dragged by their owners to the next errand.

On the far corner of Rue Saint-Honoré, I noticed the delightful exchange of friends chatting at the outdoor bistro, leisurely enjoying their morning espresso, not noticing the hustle of the world around them. Cameras flashed on each city street as tourists captured their perfect Parisian photo. It felt like a splendid day for a bike ride around town. After all, it was Sunday, our day of leisure in Paris, and what was a girl to do but play tourist for the day?

My first stop was visiting my *grand-père* who was reading *Le Figaro*, his favorite Sunday paper, on his preferred bench in the Luxembourg Gardens. We sat together as I tried to catch a glimpse of the articles he was reading. He always seemed so engrossed in the news of the day, but today he appeared more interested in my company.

"Vivienne," my grandfather asked, "do you remember a time when you felt most alive, full of spirit, zestful, and sparkling with enthusiasm?"

"Well . . ." I wondered, "No. I can't recall, Papy."

When was the last time my heart skipped a beat? When was the last time I felt true happiness unique to me? Hmmmm . . . wondered Vivienne.

"I'd like you to ride through Paris, go to your usual favorite places, but this time, take notice of what your heart and body tell you," Papy shared.

I set my itinerary in my mind. I hopped on my mint green bike, equipped with a basket on the front in case I found some treasures along my way. Perhaps I would bump into my regular Sunday crowd: Fifi at Fifi's Fleurs, Laurent at the Opera House, Charlotte at my favorite *boulangerie*, Ava at the yummiest cheese shop in all of Paris, and, of course, Dean at Borsalino's Hat Shoppe.

As I began my adventure, my stomach grumbled with hunger. The bumpy cobblestone streets made my stomach rumble for the warm goodness of Charlotte's French bread. Wafting from around the bend, I could just taste it on the tip of my tongue. "Bonjour, Charlotte! I've come for my usual Sunday morning croissant."

As I bit into Charlotte's croissant, I tasted the buttery beauty and noted its particular goodness that morning. I smiled. My tummy was happy. I really *tasted* it in all its glory.

The Palais Garnier, Paris's most famous opera house, was just around the corner. Surely Laurent was standing outside greeting guests for the Sunday matinee. Perhaps he would let me in for a sneak peak of today's ballet performance, *Le Parc*, just until intermission. "Bonjour Laurent," I said with an affectionate smile. "Is there an extra seat for me this morning?"

"Why, of course! *Oui oui mon cheri.* For you, yes," replied Laurent.

"Oh *merci* Laurent, I will not overstay my welcome," I reassured him.

The entrance of the Palais Garnier took my breath away. Its gold-drenched decor and marble-covered walls, floors, and pillars made me feel like the prima ballerina of the show! The graceful movements of the dancers and the violins playing in the background not only touched my heart but made it flutter. I *heard* the violins in a way I had never heard them before. All in unison, their melodies took my body on a quest. I immediately felt the calm, the grace, and the treasure of dance and music.

After leaving the opera house, it was time for a snack. Ah yes, Ava at Fromagerie Laurent Dubois was a necessary stop in one of my favorite neighborhoods: Saint-Germain-des-Prés. At this point, riding my bike seemed to draw my attention more so than any other day. Peddling over the centuries-old stone streets flagged my eye, and I felt the breeze through my hair with a sense of freedom and delight.

As I walked in, the *waft* of every type of cheese immediately hit me; an undoubtedly good hit. A pungent *scent* I had never noticed before. *"Un coin de brie s'il vous plait."* (A wedge of Brie?) I delightfully asked. I couldn't wait to sink my teeth into this creamy, decadent treat. I just wish I had some leftover croissant from Charlotte's boulangerie stashed away. My taste buds *burst* with happiness, and my nose journeyed through the scents of the regions! "Merci Ava," I beamed.

I continued on to my most beloved hat shop in all of Paris: Borsallino on 6 Rue de Grenelle. Its vintage green storefront draws me in each time I pass by. Hats in all textures and colors grabbed my attention. Today, I noticed the fall-inspired fabrics of tweed, wool, straw, leather, and velvet. Their colors in hues of mustard, olive, teal, and winter white were displayed so beautifully in the window.

"Bonjour, Vivienne!" echoed a voice from the back of the store. *"Voulez-vous essayer un chapeau?"* (Would you like to try on a hat?) asked Dean, the dapper-dressed, charming shopkeeper. I couldn't resist but *touch* how soft and fine these fabrics felt in my hands. Some felt fuzzy, furry, and soft, while others were shiny, rough, crisp, and smooth. The made-to-measure fedora and the straw and felt chapeaux were splendid gifts to bring to Papy. I went with the soft and fuzzy winter-white fedora for my grand-père. "Merci Dean!"

Last, but definitely not least, was Fifi's Fleur's. A bouquet to bring home to *maman* was a surefire way to plant a smile on her face to conclude the day. I peddled all the way to Rue Henry Monnier in the 9th Arrondissement to gather a *bouquet de fleurs*. I was starting to feel different since my talk with Papy earlier that morning. The more I noticed my senses, the greater joy I felt in my heart and body. I was amazed how different I felt doing the same things I did every Sunday.

"Bonjour Vivienne! *"Comment puis-je vous aider aujourd'hui?"* (How can I help you today?) Fifi asked. Before I could respond, the fragrant perfume of sweet peas, peonies, garden roses, snapdragons, irises, and lilies *filled* my nose. I slowly walked to the back of the shop, passing every color of the rainbow.

My heart skipped a beat. I couldn't think of anything else but how glorious it was to be surrounded by the sweet smells, colors, textures, and delicate blooms that all came from the earth. I was in heaven, and my body was doing flips inside. I embraced Fifi. "This is it!" I gleefully shouted.

"What's 'it'?" replied Fifi.

"This. All of this. This is exactly what Papy was referring to!"

Fifi looked at me with peculiar eyes. I was bursting with jubilation.

"My grand-père asked me if I had ever felt that zeal, zest, and spark. I hadn't until NOW."

Flowers, *the sight, the smells,* and the beauty that surrounded me covered my skin in goose bumps.

So grateful for my enthusiasm, Fifi filled my heart and mind with knowledge about flowers, and one in particular that meant a great deal to the city of Paris: the iris.

"The iris *(Iris xiphium)* symbolizes hope, cherished friendship, and valor, and is the inspiration for the Fleur-de-lis, which symbolizes the royal family of France," she noted.

She proceeded to share with me how she found her love of flowers: "Flowers are linked to a person's happiness, both immediate and long-term. Flowers can make you happy by triggering your happy brain chemicals: dopamine, serotonin, and oxytocin." My mouth hurt from the permanent smile planted on my face.

Fifi elaborated that flowers each have their own meaning and symbolism. Roses represent love, daisies represent happiness, and lilies represent support or healing. Her commentary on flowers and all that these blooms represent truly sent me soaring with appreciation and love for what I was seeing and smelling.

"Please prepare your prettiest bouquet of seasonal blooms for my *maman*," I eagerly requested. I couldn't wait to run home and share my revelation! Oh, and a pit stop at the twinkling Eiffel Tower with my blooms tucked neatly in my basket was in order.

What a Sunday! *Au Revoir!*

About the Author

Entrepreneur, first-generation American, writer, and mother to four children, María strives to bring passion and enthusiasm to all her endeavors. A lover of all things European, María has found great passion through her travels to Paris, Italy, Spain, and South America. Her affection for winemaking, foreign languages, the arts, ballroom dancing, and traveling has given María a unique and grateful perspective on life. Her love for her family and helping others through charitable giving has enabled María to thoughtfully curate purposeful life adventures.

María Castellucci Moore earned her bachelor of arts degree in finance from Dominican University on a tennis scholarship, and later pursued studying at New York University and the London School of Economics with a focus on global affairs. In 2016, with her siblings, María founded Castellucci Napa Family, a luxury wine and real estate brand. María runs her wine label and a family real estate development company in the greater Bay Area. She is a board member of the San Francisco Opera Guild and is enthusiastic about building opportunity and community through the arts.

María resides in Saint Helena, California, with her husband and four young children. She enjoys writing; traveling; attending the opera, ballet, and symphony; flower arranging; winemaking; ballroom dancing; and playing tennis and the piano.